W9-CFB-522

ROBINSON CRUSOE

DANIEL DEFOE

PLAYMORE PUBLISHERS®

Editor: Heather Hammonds
Cover Illustration: Terry Riley
Illustrations: Gilly Marklew
Typesetting: Midland Typesetters

 Robinson Crusoe
First published in 2008 by
Playmore Inc., Publishers,
58 Main Street, Hackensack, N.J. 07601

Printed in China.

The Author
Daniel Defoe (1660–1731)

Daniel Defoe, the son of a prosperous London candlemaker, grew up to become a soldier, traveler, businessman, king's friend, spy, and a writer of more than five hundred books, and other works.

He was arrested on several occasions for debt and also faced imprisonment for some of his political writings, and beliefs.

He even escaped the hangman's noose after being pardoned for supporting royal rebels against the King.

Defoe's *Robinson Crusoe* (1719) was one of the most popular novels of its time. It is thought to be based on the story of a real life Englishman who was marooned on a desert island for five years.

His other successful novels included *Moll Flanders* and *Roxana*. Defoe also wrote a popular guidebook to Britain, *A Tour Through the Whole Island of Great Britain.*

Contents

Chapter 1
Runaway

Oh, why was I so stubborn? Why didn't I listen to my father's advice? On my sixteenth birthday, I boastfully told him that I wanted to go to sea and earn my fortune.

"Young Master Robinson Crusoe," he warned, "nothing but disaster will come of it. Take a good office job in town, my boy. That's the place for you. Go to sea and you'll be shipwrecked in some uncharted land, and eaten by wild beasts or cannibals."

What did I care about wild beasts or cannibals? I was young and my heart was set on a great adventure. I was reckless and hot-blooded, and wanted to see the world.

My home was near an ancient seaport called Hull, on the east coast of England. There was never a day passed when I didn't walk down to the docks, to see which new ships had arrived from exotic places around the world.

Each time I saw a ship depart, my heart

always went with it. So my mind was made up.

My father said he would never give me permission to go, no matter how I tried to persuade him to change his mind. My mother also begged me to forget my wild dreams.

"You'll break my heart if you go," she cried. "I shall die of worry."

But I was a typically selfish young man. I was more interested in living my dreams than thinking of my parents. If they wouldn't let me go, I would run away.

My chance came sooner than I expected. I was walking along by the docks one day, when I met an old school friend. His father was captain of a ship that carried goods around the world.

"We're on our way to London to pick up a cargo for the Americas," said my friend. "My father needs another young man to help on the voyage. He'll pay you well."

It was a dream come true for me. I didn't run home to tell my parents. I knew they would never let me go. Instead, I lied to my friend's father and said my family had agreed to let me travel with him.

So I went aboard the ship on the evening of

Walking down to the docks

August 5, 1651. It was the beginning of a great romantic adventure, or so I thought.

That evening the ship raised sail and slipped away from Hull, with the sinking sun at our backs.

If only I had listened to father's warning. If only . . .

Chapter 2
Stormy Seas

Our ship sailed out into the North Sea and headed south for London, our first port of call. We had only been at sea a couple of hours when a great wind sprang up, whipping up huge waves.

My childhood dreams of adventure and excitement in foreign lands had always been filled with pictures of sun, and warm tropical oceans.

I was not prepared for my first storm in the chilly North Sea.

I was terrified, as the ship rose and fell between the stormy waves. The higher the waves, the sicker I became. I clung onto the side of the ship for dear life, the sea lashing my face with salt water.

"This is nothing," shouted my friend above the howling, screaming winds. "Wait till we get into the great oceans of the world. Then you'll know what a real storm is!"

"But this is a real storm," I protested.

"Storm! Huh!" he answered, with a grin. "Why, it's just a puff of wind on a pond."

I was sick all the way to London. I had never felt so pleased to set foot on dry land again.

I had never been to London before. What an exciting place it was. The port was full of ships from all over the world. Hardly anyone seemed to be speaking in English.

It was in London that my life took another twist. Somehow, my friend's father found out that I had run away from home.

"Go back to your parents, you foolish lad!" he said, angrily. "You are not a seafaring man. I saw how sick you were in the storm. Go home now. If you don't, your life will be full of nothing but disasters."

He was repeating my father's warning.

In truth, at that moment, I would have happily returned home to the comforts of my family life, and the love of my mother and father. But I was too proud. My friends all knew of my plans to run away. I imagined how they would laugh at me if I returned.

That evening I collected my few possessions from the ship, said goodbye to my friend, and wandered off alone. I had no idea what I

"Why, it's just a puff of wind on a pond!"

was going to do. I had nowhere to sleep and no friends. Then a sailor spotted me.

"Hey, you look a fine sailor, young lad," he said. "Are you looking for a ship to sail the seven seas?"

I had no choice now. My path in life seemed set. "Yes, sir," I answered.

The next minute, I was aboard an ancient old boat bound for Africa and the Canary Islands with a cargo of tools, clothes, and household goods.

We set sail on the morning tide and made our way down the English Channel, with a fresh breeze behind us. At first, I felt lonely and sad. I wondered if I would ever see my parents and sister again.

But the seas were smooth, the weather warm, and there was good company to be had on board. Before long, I had forgotten all about my family—and my first storm.

Once out of the Channel, we turned south for the Bay of Biscay. I had never heard of this great area of sea, which lies off the coasts of Spain and France. I didn't know it could be one of the stormiest places on earth.

A few days later, we entered the waters of the Bay. And what a storm it put on for me!

The skies darkened, and the rain fell in torrents. The wind howled through the rigging. The ship climbed up the side of one massive wave, and then surfed down the other, into valleys of deep, black water.

It heeled over at angles that terrified me. I was sure it was going to capsize. At times, I looked up from the deck and saw mountainous seas, raging high above me.

I knew this was a real storm because I saw the looks of fear on the faces of the other seamen.

At the height of the tempest I was shaking so much with fear that I had to ask permission to go below, and hide in my cabin. That didn't help. The tossing and turning of the ship made me feel even sicker.

The stormy weather lasted for two weeks, with barely a break. The strong winds blew us south at a tremendous pace.

Yet, when the clouds finally lifted and the sun returned, all the terror of the past seven days was soon forgotten. For there, just thirty miles off, lay the coastline of the great continent of Africa. What excitement for a young lad like me!

So close, and yet so far . . .

We were still some distance from shore

I was sure the ship was going to capsize.

when a member of the crew shouted from the crow's nest, the lookout at the top of the main mast.

"Ship ahoy!" he cried.

I looked up and saw him take out his telescope, and look toward the west.

"Pirates!" he screamed down to us. "It's a pirate ship!"

Chapter 3
Pirates!

As soon as the pirates saw us, they turned to give chase. We thought we could get to the safety of the shore before they reached us. But the pirate ship was much faster than ours.

The terrors of the storm were nothing, compared with the fear we felt as the pirates came closer. As their ship sailed toward us, we saw she was a large and well-armed vessel with at least fifteen cannons. The decks were swarming with pirates, all armed to the teeth.

Our ship only had five guns. We knew we would be no match for our deadly pursuer.

"Throw the cargo overboard to lighten our load!" shouted our captain. "We'll be able to go faster."

We all helped to throw the cargo overboard. The ship did begin to move a little faster through the water, especially when the captain ordered every sail to be raised.

It was still not enough. The pirate ship

The pirates came closer.

charged through the waves, coming ever closer.

"To the guns," yelled our captain. "We'll have to fight! Load the cannons, pistols, and muskets!"

The captain ordered the man steering our ship to make a sharp turn into the wind, to try and put us behind the pirates and out of their line of fire.

As we crossed their stern, he gave the order. "Fire!"

Our first volley of cannon and musket balls had the pirates ducking for cover.

"See them running scared now!" cried the captain, encouraging us on.

We had caused mayhem on the pirate ship's decks, but almost immediately, their ship turned too. Now the pirates were sailing alongside us, about a hundred yards distant.

We were still reloading our cannons when we received the full blast of at least seven of their guns. Cannon balls whistled around our ears, ripping through our sails, and bringing our main mast crashing to the deck.

It was our turn to duck. Every time we raised our heads, a deadly volley of musket shot clattered through the rigging, cutting down any poor sailor in the way.

The next time we looked up, we saw that the

pirate ship was almost within reach of our decks. This was a dreadful sight, indeed. We saw the faces of the pirates, and a more bloodthirsty lot you never did see!

As soon as their ship was alongside ours, they leapt aboard, screaming and shouting terrible oaths.

That was the most terrifying moment of my life. I had a cutlass in my belt. I whipped it out and prepared to defend myself.

I saw a pirate swinging across from the pirate ship to ours. His eyes were fixed on me. I suddenly realized that there was no escape now. This man, already bloodied across the face from our first volley of shot, was about to kill me if I didn't stop him.

It was either him or me now.

Our cutlasses clashed. He ducked and dived, avoiding my attacks. I swerved left and right, dodging his thrusts. I began to gain confidence. I realized with surprise, that I was a better swordsman than him.

We battled for several minutes, and I finally caught him a cutting blow on the shoulder. He screamed with pain, dropped his cutlass, and fell back overboard into the sea. I never saw him again.

15

The pirates leapt aboard.

Pirates!

There was no time to congratulate myself. Another pirate was on me in a moment.

I killed at least two pirates that day and we all put up a good fight. But there were too many of them for us. We were forced to surrender in the end.

Chapter 4
A Life of Slavery

We were taken prisoner aboard the pirate ship.
The next day we reached the Canary Islands.
We were led ashore, bound hand and foot with
ropes.

We soon learned our fate. We were taken to
a slave market and sold off to another pirate
captain, as crew for his ship. There was nothing
we could do — no way to escape.

Out at sea again, we discovered what a cruel
ship he ran. We were put in chains. The pirates
threatened to beat us with a cat o' nine tails, a
whip with nine lashes, if we didn't do exactly as
we were told.

It was a tough life. If there was no wind for
the sails, we had to row the boat. We were given
barely enough food and water to survive.

None of us had any idea of our destination.
We could only guess. I thought that perhaps we
were heading out across the Atlantic, toward
South America.

A Life of Slavery

"You slaves will never see your homes again," the pirate captain told us, with a sneer. "We'll use you until you are too old to work and then we'll maroon you on an island. The crows will eat what's left of you."

I spent my seventeenth birthday on that ship. I never had a sadder day.

Three weeks later, we spotted land. It gave those of us who were prisoners hope. Perhaps we would be allowed ashore. Oh, how I longed to be on land again!

It was a tough life.

But unkindly old Neptune, the God of the Sea, had other plans for us.

On August 21, 1652, a great storm hit us. The hurricane-force winds blew us in whatever direction they chose. The land came closer and closer, and the sea became shallower and shallower.

There was a horrifying crack, as the ship's rudder finally hit an underwater rock and broke away. The jolt brought down the main mast too. It broke into several pieces, narrowly missing me as it fell.

Now everyone was on their knees, praying to be saved. At last, one kindly pirate released us from our chains.

"You'll die anyway in this storm," he cried. "None of us will get to shore alive."

The wind and waves were getting more and more powerful as we stared in horror at the rocky shore awaiting us.

I heard shouts of despair, as other members of the crew saw the rocks ahead. They knew they were doomed—that the ship would be broken into a thousand pieces.

I saw a great wave coming up behind us. It pushed us high into the air and, as it passed beneath us, we dropped down with an almighty

"You'll die in this storm."

crash, and hit the rocks below.

The ship shuddered to a dreadful and sudden halt. Most of the pirates and crew were thrown into the sea and sucked beneath the waves.

The last few members of the crew still aboard must have drowned as the ship finally turned on its side, trapping them underneath.

That was the moment when I was thrown into the sea. I felt myself sinking, and struggled to keep my head above the water. I was drowning.

My last thought before I passed out was how I wished I had listened to my father's advice.

Chapter 5
Safe Ashore

I regained consciousness and found myself bobbing on the surface of the stormy sea, gasping for breath.

There was no sign of any of my fellow crewmen, so I looked around to find my bearings. It was then that I saw another mountainous wave, with spray blowing from its top, racing toward me.

I was certain this would be the end of me. The wave was too big to swim through. I waited for it to crash over me and send me to my maker.

In a last desperate attempt to stay alive, I took a great gulp of air.

Then the wave hit.

There was a roar in my ears as it turned me upside down and sucked me in. The power of the wave was so strong that I tumbled helplessly over and over, inside it.

I must have been sucked down at least ten

The wave was too big to swim through.

feet. All I could hear was the booming sound of the waves crashing high above me.

I knew I couldn't hold my breath much longer. My lungs were about to burst. Then a strong change in the current caught hold of me, and seconds later, I shot back out onto the surface of the raging sea.

I sucked in huge mouthfuls of air, coughing and spluttering, my lungs in agonizing pain. At last the coughing stopped. Gradually, the pain eased.

I heard another roar and turning onto my back, I saw to my horror that some way out still, yet another great wave was racing in toward me.

I turned over again and started to swim toward the shore. I swam with every last ounce of my strength, my arms desperately flailing to escape the raging wave.

I searched the shore for a safe place to land, but it seemed to be just one continuous line of sharp rocks. Huge black cliffs loomed up behind them.

Then the big wave finally caught up with me. It picked me up just like the first one had, and then sucked me into its whirling depths. I don't remember anything else. My mind went blank

Swimming toward the shore

and I was unconscious for a second time.

When I awoke, I found that a miracle had happened. The wave had thrown me onto a narrow band of sandy beach with vicious rocks on either side. If it had put me down just a few feet on either side, I would have been dashed to pieces.

As it was, I had a gash on my forehead and my head was bleeding.

I slowly got to my feet. Dripping wet and cold, I stumbled up the narrow beach. I looked back, but saw no sign of any living soul.

I would have waited for a while to recover my strength before climbing the cliff behind the beach. But I could see a whole series of mammoth waves still rolling in toward me. If the tide was coming in, I would not be safe from them.

There seemed to be some sort of pathway up the cliff. I took it and slowly, step by weary step, climbed to the top.

Once there, I faced the wind roaring in from the sea. But I was so happy to be safe on land. It was a miracle I was still alive!

Chapter 6
Back on the Ship

I looked out to sea, expecting to see other members of the crew being washed ashore. But there was no sign of anyone, dead or alive.

I did see an occasional sad hat bobbing on the water, or odd shoes floating by. All my fellow slaves and the pirates had drowned. I was alone.

I looked out to the remains of the ship. It was still being tossed about by the waves. How was it possible that only I had got ashore? I thanked God for my luck.

I saw that the cliffs I had climbed dropped down into a sandy cove, a little farther down the coast. Wearily, I set off towards the cove.

By the time I got there, I was feeling more alone than ever. I had seen no sign of human life anywhere.

I sat on the beach and, feeling absolutely miserable, peered sadly out to sea. The ship was twisting and turning in its death throes. At least the storm was beginning to calm down a little.

I looked out to sea.

Evening was starting to fall. I shivered. My clothes were still dripping wet. I felt desperately hungry but I was beginning to think that there was more chance of me being eaten by wild beasts that finding any food.

I certainly had no weapon to defend myself. I felt in my pockets, but all I found was my small pocketknife. I shivered again.

Night wasn't far away. I couldn't see anywhere offering shelter nearby, except a large tree behind the cove. I walked over and saw that it might be a place to sleep, so I climbed up and wedged myself into a fork of the tree.

I was so miserable. I wouldn't have worried if I had dropped from the tree whilst I was asleep, breaking my neck. That would have been a quick end to my misery.

I was so exhausted that I slept very deeply, in spite of my awkward position in the tree. When I awoke, it was daylight. The sun was climbing into the sky and the sea was just a gentle swell. It was already warm, and the storm had passed.

Then I saw the ship! It had come to rest on its side, just a few hundred yards from the beach. All its masts had been broken and swept away. The final gusts of the storm must have blown it almost ashore.

I still felt exhausted but I had always been a strong swimmer. So I waded into the water and swam out to the ship. The tropical sea was like a warm bath, and I could hardly believe how calm it had become.

The water around the ship was quite deep, so I swam around until I found a rope hanging over the side. I pulled myself up and clambered onto the sloping deck.

Holding onto whatever I could to stop myself falling over, I set out to explore what remained of the ship.

I was amazed. The ship had not been badly damaged below decks. The hold was full of water, but most of the cabins and storerooms were still dry—although the cupboards had emptied themselves as the ship turned over.

I found that the carpenter's tool kit, a medicine box, a small telescope, and lots of other useful things had survived the storm. There was plenty of food in the ship's galley too. I hungrily ate a loaf of bread and some ships' biscuits.

I realized that the ship still held all I needed to survive until a boat came to rescue me. I was sure it wouldn't be long before I was picked up, and returned to civilization.

I needed a boat to transport all the food and

useful items ashore, so I climbed back up to the main deck to see what I could find. Broken timbers, planks, and ropes were lying everywhere. A raft! I thought. I could make a raft from those materials.

It took me a couple of hours to collect the pieces I needed. Another hour and I had made a small raft of timbers, knotted together with ropes.

Then I hauled up the carpenter's chest. I took a sharp saw and cut a circular hole in the upper timbers of the raft. I found part of a broken mast to slot into the hole and tied a cross timber to the top of the mast.

I made a sail with a piece of cloth and short ropes. Finally, I found an oar with which to paddle my new raft.

I was proud of my work that morning. I gently lowered the craft into the water and secured it with a rope to the wreck. It floated perfectly.

Now I set about saving from the ship anything that I might find useful.

Exploring the ship

Chapter 7
Setting Up Camp

My first load consisted of the food I found.
There was bread, rice, a barrel of flour, cheeses,
and dried meats.

Thank goodness the sea was calm—there
was hardly any wind at all now. I paddled the
loaded raft towards the shore quite safely.

The tide was coming in and it carried the raft
and I a little farther down the coast than I had
intended. It was a lucky moment for me. The
tide swept me into a sheltered creek.

The raft came to a gentle stop and I went
ashore to have a look around. I had landed in
a forest clearing beside the creek. On either
side of the clearing were thick belts of trees
that closed in around a sheer cliff. There was a
small cave in the cliff.

I went into the cave and had a look around.
It was quite deep and I thought that it would
make a good place to store all the things I had
taken from the ship.

Leaving the cave, I looked out between the trees on either side of the clearing. I saw what a good view it gave me of the beach, and the sea beyond. Then, best of all, I found a spring of freshwater bubbling up at the bottom of the cliff.

What a perfect place to build a camp to await my rescue!

I unloaded my newfound treasures and then returned to the ship, to collect some more valuables. This time I saved some bags of corn, barley, and sugar.

On the way to shore again, I saw a high hill just a little way inland from where I had set up camp. It would make a good lookout.

It took three more loads to rescue all the food that had survived the shipwreck. How wonderful it was to enjoy some bread and meat after my hard work that morning.

I spent the afternoon rescuing more goods from the ship. I took clothes, bedding, some tarpaulins, medicines, cutlery, mugs and plates, pots and pans, buckets, the carpenter's toolbox, and a small telescope.

But my final load that day was as important as the food. The ship's armory was undamaged, although I had to break down the heavy locked door that protected it.

A perfect place to build a camp.

I rescued eight muskets, ten pistols, some bags of musket shot, two barrels of gunpowder, a sack of gunflints, and some cutlasses and daggers.

The sun was sinking on the western horizon by the time I returned to camp in the evening.

I hid myself under a heavy tarpaulin that night. Clouds had blown in from the sea during the evening and there was no moon to be seen. It couldn't have been any darker.

I shivered each time I heard the cry of some strange animal in the distance. But I was so exhausted that I quickly fell into a deep sleep.

I woke up the next morning and peered out from under the tarpaulin. The sun was already high in the sky and a warm tropical breeze was blowing in from the ocean.

After I had breakfasted, I set off to explore the land around me. My first aim was to climb the hill behind my camp. I took one of the muskets with me, and some gunpowder and shot, and the telescope.

The land was heavily wooded and the hill was steep. I was soon dripping with sweat, with the sun burning down on my head.

The trees and bushes on the hill seemed alive with animals and birds. I could hear their calls and cries. A little farther up, I saw a huge bird perched on a branch. I stopped and loaded my musket. I took aim and fired.

The bird dropped dead from its perch, but from every other tree and bush, hundreds of birds fluttered into the air in fright. It must have been the first gunshot to be fired in that place since the world began.

I picked up my supper and continued upward. I was almost out of breath by the time

Climbing the hill behind my camp

I finally stumbled onto the summit of the hill. Falling to my knees with exhaustion, I looked out. It didn't take me long to see what a desperate situation I had been left in by the shipwreck.

I was on an island!

I turned a complete circle and saw nothing but sea in all directions, except a tiny speck of land far away to the west. It could have been another small island or a great continent, for all I knew.

Now I was more frightened than ever.

Chapter 8
A Surprise

From the top of the hill I looked out over my island and the surrounding sea. I could see neither any sign of human life on the island nor any ships out to sea.

My heart sank, as I realized that I truly was alone on the island. I had never felt such a feeling of emptiness.

A dreadful thought suddenly came to me.

"What if no one comes to rescue me?" I whispered to myself.

The only people who knew where I was were now lying at the bottom of the sea.

No one alive knew what had become of me; least of all my poor parents. I wondered if I would be forced to spend the rest of my life marooned on the island.

From the hill, I could clearly see my camp was on the eastern side of the island. The land between my beachside camp and the west

A Surprise

"What if no one comes to rescue me?"

coast was a mix of thick tropical forest and more open areas.

Close to the western shore was another beach. The rest of the coastline appeared to be rocky and inhospitable.

Looking westward, I examined again the speck of land I had seen in the distance. I took out my telescope this time. The speck became a little larger, but still gave me no clue to whether it was an island or a continent.

I descended the hill and returned to my camp. That afternoon I set off again, to see what else I could rescue from the ship.

This time I brought back several large sails and lots of rigging ropes. I also found a sleeping hammock still swinging from a cabin roof, a fishing rod, line and hooks, and a case of candles.

It was dusk by the time I had unloaded my goods and secured the raft. I made a fire and then tried my hand at fishing. It couldn't have been easier. I soon caught myself two fine fat fish that I cleaned and then cooked.

I spent another night under the great tarpaulin. I didn't sleep much because the wind was getting up again. Soon it was howling through my camp.

A Surprise

As I lay beneath my tarpaulin I heard something else, besides the wind. A crying, whimpering sound was coming from somewhere close by. I was sure it must be some wild creature, and trembled in fear.

A little later, I heard the sound again. This time it was even closer. Then something was sniffing at the tarpaulin, where my feet lay hidden.

I froze. I heard more shuffling sounds. Something was trying to get under the tarpaulin! I was so frightened that I couldn't move a muscle.

The dreaded beast finally found a way in. At any second I expected some terrible creature to sink its fangs into me.

I felt the creature creeping up my body. At last, my frozen muscles moved. My body jerked violently. I gasped. I heard a yelp. Then something started licking my nose.

It was Rosie, the pirate leader's dog!

Somehow Rosie must have got ashore when the ship was wrecked.

You cannot imagine how delighted I was to have found a companion. And I was sure the poor little creature was as happy to have found me too.

Rosie curled up beside me and fell asleep.

I dozed off after a while too, feeling happier than I had in days.

I awoke the next morning to find Rosie licking my nose again. She wouldn't let me out of her sight, and followed me everywhere.

I was now beginning to accept the fact that perhaps rescue wasn't going to come immediately—if ever. I decided that I must keep a record of the days. I knew that my ship had been wrecked on August 21, 1652, almost exactly a year after leaving my home in England.

I made a post from a dead branch and stuck it into the ground. Using my penknife, I cut three notches to mark my first three days. I intended to cut a notch every morning. That way I could be sure of the day and the month.

The next thing I did was to set about building myself a proper camp from the materials I had found on the ship.

I was about to start work when I looked out across the beach. Something was wrong. Something had changed. For a moment, I wasn't sure what. Then I suddenly realized what had happened.

A Surprise

It was Rosie!

Chapter 9
Castle Crusoe

The ship had vanished!

The night's storm must have lifted her off the rocks and carried her out to sea. I was sad to see her gone. Apart from Rosie, the ship was my last connection with my old life.

But I was so glad that I had taken everything useful from her. Now I set about using those things, to make myself safer and more comfortable.

The cave in the cliff had already become my storehouse. Now I cut several strong tree branches and built a framework, outside its entrance. I covered this with one of the ship's sails. It made a perfect waterproof tent.

I slung the ship's hammock between the tent's two main poles and was well pleased, as I would no longer have to sleep on the ground.

My tent was very comfortable indeed!

Over the next few weeks, I added to my work. Outside my new home, I made a ramshackle

A perfect waterproof tent

table and chair from bits of old ship's timbers.

I also built a kitchen area with a fireplace dug into the ground. I had rescued a large cooking pot from the ship, and this provided me with many a good fish stew.

I made a second framework of branches and stretched another sail over them, so that my kitchen area was protected from the rains.

Next, I set about putting some defenses around my new home. I felt certain that I was alone on the island, but as I hadn't visited every corner of it, I couldn't be sure.

That worried me. I was very frightened by the idea of being attacked by some, as yet, unseen enemy. Perhaps they were already watching me, waiting for the right moment to attack.

So I set about defending my castle, as I came to call my camp. The camp was already protected to the rear by the cliff face. No one could attack me from that direction.

I now sat down at the front of my tent, to puzzle out how to defend myself from any assault from the beach. This was the only direction my camp could be attacked from.

I decided to build a fence with sharply-pointed stakes in front of it; a sort of stockade made of stakes. The stockade would curve in a semi-circle around my camp and link up with the cliff.

First, I cut some strong, straight branches from the nearby woodland with the carpenter's saw. I used the axe to sharpen one end of each. Some I drove into the ground to make the stockade. Others I used as stakes pointing toward the beach.

I planted the sharpened stakes so close to each other that no man could get through safely. In any case, no one would dare risk trying to climb over those spikes, knowing that I might also be firing my muskets.

I still wasn't happy. My castle needed something else. I asked myself what else an English castle would have . . . of course, a moat! Or at any rate, a ditch.

But how could I dig a ditch without a spade? That was one thing I hadn't found on the ship.

Carpentry was not one of my skills, but making a spade proved not to be as difficult as I imagined.

I cut a block of timber from a fallen tree trunk and set about carving it to shape with my axe. It took me a whole week to make, but the tool made life much easier.

Over the next month I dug a deep ditch right

A fence of sharply-pointed stakes

around the front of the stockade. It would take a determined person or wild animal to break into my castle now, I thought.

There was no gate or doorway through my defenses. Instead, I made two ladders—one to climb over the defenses into the camp, and another to climb out. At night I would bring both the ladders into the camp with me.

As more weeks passed, I gradually came to feel quite safe behind my ditch and stockade. And then the most unexpected thing happened. Some of the stakes I had cut from living trees began to grow new shoots. Day by day, they got taller and thicker.

I could see that one day, they would completely hide my home from anyone on the beach.

Chapter 10
Counting My Blessings

I built a large bonfire on top of the big hill, which I called Beacon Hill. I planned to light the bonfire to alert any passing ships to my presence.

I soon developed a daily routine in my life on the island.

I started each day by climbing Beacon Hill to search the horizons for any sign of a ship. Then after breakfast, I went out with my musket to shoot birds for my cooking pot.

To my delight, I discovered that wild goats roamed the island. I only needed to shoot one a week to give myself a good food supply.

I always made sure I was home by late afternoon. At that time of day I made my second visit to Beacon Hill, to look out for ships.

Evening was the time for thunderstorms on this tropical island. It was the heat of the day that brought them on. Black clouds swept in from the sea. Thunder rumbled around the

Building a bonfire

island and lightning flashed across the sky. Then the rain would start to fall in torrents.

Rosie always ran and hid in the cave when the storms came. But they never lasted long. The peace of the evening soon descended on the island and the sun returned for a short while.

Birdsong and the surf rolling onto the beach were often the only sounds to be heard as I cooked my evening meal. Afterwards, I would watch the sun set.

Sometimes I would take a late walk along the beach beneath the stars with Rosie. Yet, despite her company, I still felt dreadfully lonely and homesick. I thought of my parents and sister a lot.

One day, to cheer myself up, I took a stick and wrote in the sand a list of all the good and bad things about life on the island.

Bad	*Good*
I am trapped on an unknown island.	*I didn't drown like the others.*
I am alone.	*I alone survived the shipwreck.*
I am separated from my family.	*I have Rosie for company.*

The poor in England go hungry.	*I am never hungry on the island.*
I haven't many clothes.	*I don't need many clothes on a hot tropical island.*
I have no one to speak to.	*Rosie understands me.*

And so, I counted my blessings. I decided life on the island was better than being drowned like the others.

And so, I counted my blessings.

55

But as the days and weeks passed, I became more and more certain that I would never see another ship again. I was sure I was doomed to live on the island until I died a lonely death in my tent.

I wondered if anyone would ever find my skeleton.

Chapter 11
My First Year

How time passed! It came as quite a surprise to me when I carved my 365th notch on my calendar pole. I had been on the island for a year!

I could hardly believe it. I was now eighteen years old. I wondered what my parents would be thinking now. Perhaps they thought me dead.

If they had seen me then, they would never have recognized me. Most of my face was covered with a long beard that stretched down onto my chest, and I was deeply tanned from the sun.

My clothes had fallen into tatters in that first year. I had managed to make some new but very rough clothes, from the skins of goats I had killed.

But if I was a bad carpenter, I was a worse tailor. The knee-length breeches I made flapped around my legs. They were held up by a strip of old goat skin.

I also made a kind of sleeveless waistcoat and a very odd-looking cap, with a flap hanging down my neck for protection from the sun.

In my belt I always carried a cutlass and loaded pistol, and also my carpenter's saw and axe, if I needed them. Another belt went over my chest and across my shoulder. Attached to that were bags for my powder, shot, and gun-flints.

There was one other item of which I was very proud. I made an umbrella to help keep the worst of the sun off me. It had a device that let me raise and lower it.

All in all, I must have been a very strange sight.

***

On that first anniversary, the sun was burning down as usual. I decided to go for a swim to cool down. At times, the solitude and beauty of my surroundings took away the pain of being so alone.

I swam out a little way and turned on my back to float for a while. It was so relaxing in the warm water that I almost fell asleep.

Then something brought me back to life. It

I had been on the island for a year!

was an instinctive feeling. I felt I was not alone anymore.

I flopped over to look back to the beach. No, the beach was as empty as ever. I was about to roll onto my back again when I caught sight of something far out to sea. It was moving!

I swam to shore as fast as I could and grabbed my telescope. I anxiously searched the horizon. Perhaps it had been just a distant cloud. I couldn't see anything at first. Then, there it was! A ship! It was big vessel, with all sails flying in the wind.

I screamed out aloud. What a fool I was! The ship must have been a mile or more way. No one would hear me.

I raced off the beach and sped up Beacon Hill. I quickly lit the beacon with sparks from a flint. The firewood was bone dry and quickly burst into flames.

Nearby, I had a pile of new leaves that I had kept damp. I threw these on the fire and soon it was billowing dark smoke into the sky.

I don't know why, but I kept waving my arms too, in an effort to attract the attention of those on the ship. Of course, no one could ever have seen me from that distance.

I looked through my telescope again. Were

A ship!

my eyes deceiving me or had the ship made a
change of course? Had it seen my beacon? Was
I to be rescued at last?

My hopes fell. The ship hadn't changed
course—it was still sailing away from me.
I watched it as it grew smaller and smaller. I
wondered if it was an English ship. It looked
like one, but I couldn't make out the flag on its
main mast.

It was dusk when it finally disappeared over
the horizon.

I sat down and cried like a child.

Chapter 12
Farmer Crusoe

It took me a long time to get over the sight of that ship. Another year passed and I saw no other, though I searched the horizon from Beacon Hill every day.

Yet for every unhappy moment on the island, there was one of hope too.

One day I found water had got into one of the sacks of corn I had rescued from the ship. Part of it had gone rotten, so I just threw it onto my rubbish pile outside the stockade.

To my astonishment, a few days later I saw that some of the grains of corn had sprouted shoots. The hot sun by day and regular evening rainfall must have made perfect growing conditions.

Within weeks, those first shoots had grown into new ears of corn. I picked off the ears and rubbed them between my hands. From those few grains of rotten corn, fifty new grains had now grown.

I was so happy. I knew that I could plant these and produce even more. With a little luck, in time I might produce enough to make flour. My own stock of flour from the ship had long run out. How I had missed the bread that I made with it!

***

After I discovered that I could grow corn, I began to plan more for the future. If the island was to be my home for a long time, then I must think ahead.

One morning, as I was exploring a part of the island I had never seen before, I stumbled into a wonderful valley hidden away in the center of the island. I reached it by walking through a narrow chasm.

Inside, the valley was surrounded by a circle of rocky hills. There was a crystal clear stream running though it and its slopes were covered with orange trees, and coconut palms. I saw plums, grapes, and other fruits growing there too.

Perhaps the hot sun had gone to my head; I started thinking that if I already had my own castle on the coast, why couldn't I have a farm in the country as well?

Farmer Crusoe

The grains of corn had sprouted.

So I surveyed the valley and discovered some flat meadows beside the stream. They would suit my purposes perfectly.

Over the next few days, I built my farmhouse. It was very similar to my home on the coast—a ship's sail thrown over a strong framework of wooden branches.

The next part of the operation was more difficult. I had no plough, of course. So I had to start off by digging my first planting area with the spade. Fortunately, the soil wasn't too hard to work.

In this beautiful place I planted my fifty grains of corn, and some young orange and plum trees.

I loved staying at my farm. The valley was such a beautiful, quiet place. I called it Valley Farm. I spent many days working and sleeping on my farm, although I always hurried back to look out from Beacon Hill at least once a day.

My diet was getting better all the time. I now had fruit juice from fresh oranges or coconuts for breakfast. There was roast goat for lunch. And for my evening meal, I would poach turtle eggs that I found on the beach.

Now that my gunpowder and ammunition was getting a little short, I knew I had to find

Valley Farm

another way of keeping my supply of goats' meat.

Rosie gave me the answer. One morning she went hunting, and returned to the farm with a tiny goat kid in her mouth. It was still alive.

I realized that I could capture a few more goats and breed them on the farm. So I made a wooden trap. Then I placed it on one of the tracks that I had seen the goats use.

I caught nothing in the first week. But in the second I caught a large male Billy goat, two young females, and three kids. I moved them all into a small enclosure I had made on the farm.

The Billy goat was the wildest creature I ever saw on the island, though he soon calmed down when he realized that I was going to feed him every day. The others became tame very quickly, too.

It was a very successful project for me. The Billy goat and the females quickly bred, and had more young.

Now, I not only had a good supply of goats' meat to eat, but I also learned to milk the females. I was so successful that I set up a small dairy hut by the goats' enclosure. Some of the milk I drank, and the rest I turned into butter and cheese.

I settled into my new life, spending my time between my castle and farm.

I couldn't say I was happy to be trapped alone on a deserted island. Yet, Rosie was a good companion and I was becoming increasingly confident that there was no one else on the island. I had nothing to fear.

As each year passed I felt safer and safer. I wasn't to know then, how quickly things were to change.

Chapter 13
A Fearful Earthquake

The first rumble of approaching danger came as I was nearing the end of my fourth year on the island. It happened on my twenty-first birthday.

I had just had my breakfast in my castle by the beach, when Rosie began to whine. At first I thought she was ill. But there didn't seem anything wrong with her.

Suddenly, the ground began to shake beneath my feet. Trees swayed, as if someone was tugging at them by the roots. I was terrified. Rosie must have felt it coming and this was why she'd been upset.

It was an earthquake! When I was in England I had heard about these things happening in far-off places. I had no idea how frightening they would be.

I watched, as trees were uprooted and crashed to the ground. An astonishingly powerful wind sprang up, howling across the island.

It was an earthquake!

Rosie and I hid in the cave in the cliff and prayed we would survive. Even the cliff was moving and rumbling, and threatening to collapse at any minute. Then it was over, as quickly as it had begun.

I imagined the earthquake might set off a tidal wave that would engulf my island home. No tidal wave arrived, but the dreadful wind grew to hurricane force, and blew my tent away.

I spent the rest of the day in shock. The next morning I went hunting for my tent. I found it miles away down the coast.

A few days after that, I got a fever. I must have eaten some rotten fish. I couldn't stop shaking for a week, and I thought I would die without a doctor to save me. I didn't even have the strength to climb out of my hammock.

I had the strangest dreams during that fever. In one, I imagined I was Governor of my island. When I was fully recovered I thought about that feverish dream again. Why shouldn't I be Governor? I could rule the island on behalf of England, until I was rescued.

And so I appointed myself Governor of the island. But, of course, if the island had a name, I didn't know it. I decided to give the island a name myself. I quickly realized there was only one thing I could call it . . . Crusoe Island.

From now on, I would be Governor of Crusoe Island, and Master of Castle Crusoe and Valley Farm. I decided that my first job as Governor was to make sure I had surveyed the whole island. I started a series of journeys that took me to every corner.

It was on one of these journeys in my sixth year on the island, that I began to suspect that perhaps I wasn't alone after all.

I made a discovery that chilled me to the bone!

I had the strangest dreams.

Chapter 14
Into Unknown Territory

I had decided to explore the west coast. That was the side of the island nearest the speck of land I had seen far in the distance. I had never explored the west coast before, because it was the most remote part of my kingdom.

Looking from Beacon Hill, it seemed to be an area of sandy beach with a thick tropical forest, just inland.

I set off early one morning with Rosie. As usual, I carried a loaded musket and a pistol with me, just in case of trouble.

I visited Valley Farm on the way. The corn seemed to be growing well. While I was there I moved the goats into a new enclosure of grass near the stream. That way they would have plenty of food and water, in case I was away for several days.

I had no idea how long it would take me to reach the west coast. The first part of the journey was easy traveling. I made good progress and reached the edge of the tropical forest by the first evening.

I camped there, underneath a large tree. I hardly slept a wink that night, for every time I was about to nod off, some new terrifying screech or scream came from the forest.

At least I knew—or was fairly sure—that they weren't human sounds.

The next day, I set off again. Hour by hour the forest became thicker and darker. The sun hardly penetrated the forest floor at all. I traveled on in a dull green light.

The muddy swamp areas of the forest were the worst, and I had to carry Rosie across them. Sometimes I saw snakes swimming through the murky waters. Rosie snarled at them, which seemed to keep them away.

I was still not out of the forest by evening, but I managed to find a bit of raised land that was dry enough to spend the night.

Once the dim light of the sinking sun had vanished, all was complete and utter blackness. Once more the night was filled with dreadful cries and shrieks from all around me. Rosie huddled close to me, whimpering softly.

We were both happier when at last, the first faint rays of dawn filtered through the trees.

On I went. But this time the forest became lighter with each step. I was approaching the coast, and could hear the distant crash of the waves on the shore.

Suddenly I jumped with fright, as something landed on my shoulder. I turned my head to look, dreading what I might find. I was amazed to see a young red parrot perched on my shoulder, looking at me with a very inquisitive eye.

How I laughed with relief! Rosie didn't know what to make of it.

The bird was a very friendly creature, and it seemed to have no intention of leaving its perch. I gave it a pinch of my cheese, which it liked very much.

"We'll call it Poll," I said to Rosie.

We continued on and, very soon after, the three of us emerged from the forest onto a sandy beach. I was so hot after the last part of the walk. I ran to the sea, quickly followed by Rosie. Poll swooped alongside us.

I dived straight in. How wonderful that cooling water was after the hot and sticky walk through the forest. I rolled over and over in delight. Rosie was just as excited.

Afterwards, I sat in the sun until my clothes were dry and then set off to explore the beach

Hour by hour the forest became thicker.

"We'll call it Poll."

with Rosie. Poll perched on my shoulder again, squawking as if he had something to tell me.

I walked on down the beach, looking out to sea. Once more I could just make out the speck of land on the distant western horizon. Could it be the mainland of South America, I wondered.

I walked on, but I began to feel very uneasy. There was some strange, unhappy atmosphere about this beach. It was as if it had been touched by evil.

The feeling got stronger, the farther down the beach I walked. Then I saw something completely extraordinary and totally unexpected. I stopped and looked down at the sand beneath my feet.

There, planted firmly in the sand, was a human footprint!

Chapter 15
The Footprint

I stood staring down at the footprint in the sand. I had been on the island for six long years, without any sign of another human being until now. I was thunderstruck.

There was no mistaking it. There was a clear impression of a foot, showing the heel and five toes.

I couldn't think straight for a moment. I looked up and down the beach. Perhaps it was my own foot. Perhaps I had come this way when we reached the beach.

I quickly realized I had come nowhere near this spot before. I looked up and listened. I saw and heard nothing unusual. I ran up to the top of the beach, near the forest, to get a higher view of my surroundings. I slowly looked around, but saw no one.

I ran back to the footprint just to make sure I hadn't been dreaming.

No, there it was, as clear as anything. There

The footprint in the sand.

was only one footprint, and nothing else to see. Perhaps the tide had rubbed away the other one.

The print left behind was that made by a right foot. It was large—larger than mine. It must have belonged to a big man.

Suddenly, I became very frightened. What if this man was looking at me now from some forest hideaway? What if he was taking aim at me with his gun? Worse still, what if the man belonged to a tribe of cannibals, looking to me for their next meal?

I panicked. I started running. I was quickly clear of the beach and heading back into the forest with Rosie at my heels and Poll flying above.

I had never run so fast. I kept looking behind in case someone was following me.

It had taken me a day and a half to cross the forest on the way to the coast. On the way back, I raced home in less than a day. I was so frightened.

The sun was just setting by the time I reached Valley Farm. But even then, I wasn't happy. I knew I wouldn't feel safe until I was back in my castle.

It was dark by the time I finally arrived at

Castle Crusoe. I carried Rosie over the ladders and fell exhausted into my hammock.

I didn't sleep a wink that night. I couldn't rid my mind of the image of that footprint. Who owned it? How had he come to the island? Where was his boat? Was he alone, or with others?

Those questions tumbled around my head all night, and haunted my dreams for months to come.

I raced home in less than a day.

Sometimes, in the middle of the night, I managed to persuade myself that it must have been me who made the footprint. But in the morning I knew I couldn't fool myself.

I hardly went outside at all in the next few months, other than to dash to my farm to milk the goats and see they were all right.

I still climbed Beacon Hill each day, though. I always looked across to the western coast. But the view never changed. I never saw a ship, or any sign of life on the beach there.

***

Two more years passed and nothing happened, and no one appeared. I was nearly twenty-five years old.

Slowly, I began to think myself foolish. What was one small footprint? It might have been made years earlier. It might have been one of the victims of my shipwreck who managed to get ashore, and then died.

The wild animals could easily have devoured what remained of him.

Gradually, life returned to normal. On some days I didn't even think about that footprint.

My farm blossomed. The crops of corn grew

The Footprint

My farm blossomed.

85

richer in the warm, tropical climate. I harvested them with an old cutlass. Then I laid out the crop on a flat rock and beat it with sticks, until all the corn had fallen out of the ears.

I ground some corn with a stone to make flour for bread. The rest I kept back to sow as the next crop.

My latest harvest produced ten sacks of corn. After making my flour, there was enough corn left to plant an acre of ground. I understood the tropical seasons now, and I knew which months were best to plant the corn.

My goats bred well too. I soon had a fine herd of thirty or more. Of course, there had been many others that I ate.

I discovered that the birds liked my crops too. I had to build a scarecrow. That soon scared them away, although it often frightened Poll too.

Poll gave me one of the biggest thrills of my long imprisonment on the island. Because I was alone, I quite often spoke to Rosie. In the evening I'd tell her what I had done that day.

"I planted more corn today," I would say. "More bread for us."

Sometimes when I was sad, I would sigh and say, "What's to become of Robinson Crusoe, Rosie?"

I'd noticed that Poll, who still spent most of his day on my shoulder, had been squawking more than usual. Then one day, he spoke!

"What's to become of Robinson Crusoe," he chirped.

I was astounded. They were the first words I had heard from another creature for many years. I knew parrots could talk, but I never expected Poll to say anything.

In the months that followed, Poll learned lots of phrases. It was almost as if I had someone to talk with. He learned one particular sentence that I now often said to myself:

"Whose footprint? I must go back."

After all this time I convinced myself there was nothing to be frightened of. I would go back to where I had first seen the footprint. But not on foot through that awful forest again.

I decided to build a boat. I was going to sail my way round!

Chapter 16
Building a Boat

My raft had served me well, but it was certainly not a craft to go to sea in.

Building a boat would be a major project that would take some time to complete, but it was the only way I would be able to sail round the island.

My first task was to find two suitable trees. Next I spent two weeks cutting off all the branches, and then another month hacking one of the tree trunks into plank-length sections.

It took another two months to saw the sections into thin planks for the decking. Then it took three more months to carve out the inside of the trunk of the second tree. This served as the hull and interior of the boat. Laying the deck and setting the mast took a further two weeks.

In all, it took seven whole months to finish my boat, and it was a lot bigger than I had planned. There was room for ten or more people inside.

Carving out the interior of the boat

The boat was indeed a splendid craft. But hardly had I laid down my axe and chisels than I discovered my major mistake.

I had always imagined I would be able to haul the boat to the creek that led from my camp to the sea. Now, when I tried to move it, it wouldn't budge an inch.

I tried my biggest ropes and even log rollers beneath it, but it was no use. I had made the boat too heavy to move.

There was only one alternative. If I couldn't move the boat to water, I would have to bring the water to the boat.

The boat lay more than thirty yards from the creek, so I decided to dig a canal. The canal would have to be at least four feet deep and six feet wide to carry the boat to the water.

I started digging.

I dug every day for three months. It was backbreaking work.

Close to the ninth anniversary of my arriving on the island, I finally broke through. The water rushed in, and within a few minutes had filled up my canal.

My boat slipped sideways and slowly launched itself into the canal. As she lay gently bobbing up and down, I fixed a rope on her

She lay gently bobbing up and down.

bow and tied it to the nearest tree. I didn't want the tide to steal her.

I spent the next two weeks getting the boat ready for the sea. I cut out a sail and carved a wooden anchor, two oars, and a steering rudder.

I made a locker for my guns and powder, and another for food and water. I even made a small dog cabin for Rosie, and a wooden cage for Poll.

Finally, I fixed my umbrella to the stern of the boat to keep the sun off me. Then I waited for fine weather.

Setting sail for the west coast

At dawn on August 21, 1661, nine years after I had arrived on the island, Rosie, Poll, and I set out on our first voyage.

It felt wonderful, at first. The wind caught the sails and quickly pushed the boat out of the inlet. The weather was pleasant and the seas were calm.

I sailed around the south coast of the island and then headed north toward the western beach, which I had now renamed Footprint Beach.

But then things went all wrong. First, the wind started to get up.

Soon I was racing along the coast, almost out of control. I thought it was just the wind, but I was wrong.

I was now caught in a strange and powerful current that was sweeping me out toward the great ocean.

Chapter 17
All at Sea

I tried everything to regain control of my craft.
It was hopeless. Soon I was far out to sea.

I could see no way of getting back. I wished I
had never built the boat. Why did I have to go
to sea? I was quite comfortable on my island.
Why did I have to go and spoil everything?

As evening fell, the current seemed to lose
some of its power and the boat slowed right
down. By nightfall, it wasn't moving at all.

There was still nothing I could do. I sat in
the stern with Rosie at my feet and Poll on
my shoulder. Gradually the motion of the sea
rocked me to sleep.

I awoke at first light. The boat was moving
again. I dreaded even looking out to see how
much farther it had carried me away from my
island.

When I finally did, I saw that I wasn't going
farther out to sea. The tide had caught the boat

The sea rocked me to sleep.

and was pushing her back towards a headland, close to Footprint Beach.

By using the rudder and oars, I successfully beached the boat in a tiny cove close to the beach. I was never so happy to be ashore again.

That morning, I began to think about the footprint and the dot of land on the horizon. Perhaps people from that place came over by canoe to visit my island for some reason. Was that how the footprint had been made?

I found it strange that I had not seen any other signs of life, despite living on the island for nine years.

I left the boat in the cove and walked around to the beach. I found no more footprints and no signs of anyone having visited the beach again.

I did see a small pile of bones, but I thought they must have belonged to some unfortunate seaman who had been drowned at sea and washed up on my island.

I sailed back to my castle that evening without any problem. I had studied the currents from a small hill near Footprint Beach, and soon realized that they changed with the tides. Once I understood them, I felt it safe to return home.

Once more I had convinced myself that I was

alone. But I strengthened my castle defenses, just in case of visitors.

By now my home was completely hidden by the trees and bushes that had grown alongside the stockade. I set up all my weapons so that if ever I needed to, I would be able to defend myself.

I had made six shooting positions along the stockade. Each had a view through the greenery to the beach. Each also had a musket and a pistol ready for loading.

I practiced loading and firing the muskets and pistols, to see how quickly I could fire them all. I estimated that if I had time to load the muskets first, I could fire all six in less than a minute.

***

Time passed, and I marked my eleventh year on the island with a first boat trip right around it. What a momentous voyage that was.

I had sailed around the north of the island and was heading south toward Footprint Beach, when I saw something moving out to sea.

I raised my telescope to my eye and peered into the distance.

The object was so far away that I couldn't see what it was. Gradually, it vanished over the horizon. Could it have been a boat?

I was so disappointed. It unsettled me greatly. I had become used to the idea that I would spend the rest of my life on the island. But the thought of a boat in the area raised my first real hopes in years of being rescued.

I put ashore in the cove near Footprint Beach and walked over to the beach. The first thing I noticed was that the pile of bones I had seen before had grown bigger.

Now I definitely recognized some of the bones as human. Worse still, I noticed that many of the bones had been gnawed at. I also saw what looked like the remains of a fire close by.

I could not hide the truth from myself any longer. Perhaps I was alone on the island. But people had indeed visited the place since I had arrived. And they had left behind the evidence of who they were.

The people who had come unseen to my island home were cannibals!

My home was completely hidden.

Chapter 18
A Sad Death

My discovery sent shivers down my spine. I ran off the beach, quickly found my boat, and set sail again for my castle home.

I was comforted by only one fact. Whoever came to this island only ever put ashore on Footprint Beach. To my knowledge, they had never attempted to reach the east coast.

I never fired my guns after that day. I didn't want to alert anyone to my presence, if they ever came again. Luckily, I didn't need to shoot any creatures for food. There was always good fishing and I had a large herd of goats now.

I felt rather sad when I had to kill one from my herd to eat. Some of them had almost become pets to me. But I had to survive.

I stopped burning large fires and kept very quiet, too. The noisiest thing around my camp now was Poll the parrot with his constant chatter, using the words I had taught him.

"Robinson Crusoe! Robinson Crusoe!" he

"Robinson Crusoe! Robinson Crusoe!"

cried. "Where are you? Where have you been? How did you get here?"

If I did venture anywhere near the west coast, I always went well armed in case I met any visitors.

Whenever I went out into the country around my castle or farm, I now carried two loaded muskets over my shoulder, together with two pistols and a cutlass, stuck in my goatskin belt.

If anyone had seen me, I think they would have run a mile. I must have looked a terrifying creature with my weaponry and wild appearance.

Slowly I got back into my routine.

I would milk my goats first thing in the morning and then climb Beacon Hill to see if any ship was approaching. I paid special attention to the area around Footprint Beach.

Many months passed and I never saw a sign of any person or any boat.

***

On Christmas Day 1665, Rosie died. The faithful dog had given me such loyal company during our time together on the island. She had grown old and gray around the muzzle, as the years had passed.

I buried Rosie on top of Beacon Hill and built a pile of stones on her grave. She had loved it up on that hill, and would wag her tail and sniff the sea air excitedly whenever we climbed it.

I buried Rosie on top of Beacon Hill.

Oh, how I missed my friend! I often visited her grave and talked to her.

One morning, I had climbed Beacon Hill a little earlier than usual. It was almost light but the sun wasn't up yet. I searched the horizons with my telescope as usual, and saw no sign of any movement out to sea.

I was just walking over toward Rosie's grave when I saw, in the half light, the glow of a fire in the area of Footprint Beach.

My devilish visitors must have returned!

Chapter 19
Visitors!

However frightened I felt, I knew I had to go and find out who those awful visitors were.

I set sail for the west coast. The wind was against me, and it was evening by the time I dropped sail by the headland beyond the beach.

I put my boat ashore in the cove and walked to the beach. I found myself a safe hiding place just inside the forest behind the beach. I loaded my muskets and pistols and laid them out, ready to fire.

In the dull evening light I could make out three or four canoes beached on the tide line. I counted ten men sleeping around a fire.

I was horrified at what I saw next. Not far away from me, a young man was tied to a post at the back of the beach. He was surely the cannibals' next victim.

There was nothing I could do now, so I settled down to watch my unwelcome visitors.

As the hours passed I heard the wind starting to rise. A storm was racing in from the west. It began with great cracks of thunder, followed by violent flashes of lightning. The men around the fire started to stir.

I covered the muskets and pistols to keep them dry, as the rain began to fall in torrents.

Suddenly, I saw a ship. There was another great flash of lightning. Yes! I clearly saw that a large ship was passing the island, and traveling east. The ship was less than a mile out to sea. She looked like a man-of-war of the English Navy.

I wanted to leap up and down, and scream out to attract the ship's attention. But I dared not. My visitors were just a few hundred yards away.

I prayed the ship might suddenly turn and drop anchor by the island. But I watched her disappear behind the headland.

The men around the fire were wide awake now, but they had not noticed the ship. I looked over to the man tied to the tree. He was struggling with the ropes that bound him.

What was he doing?

I suddenly realized what he was up to. With a last desperate wriggle through his bonds, the man was free. He raced off, heading in my direction, toward the safety of the forest.

Suddenly, I saw a ship.

His captors saw him. There were wild screams and shouts as they leapt to their feet and gave chase.

The man raced up into bushes, where I was hiding. Suddenly, he saw me. For a moment, he stopped in his tracks. Perhaps he thought I was going to recapture him.

I used hand signals to urge him to get away while he could. He seemed to understand and raced away into the forest.

The next moment his pursuers came into view. They were an ugly, cruel-looking band of men. I didn't think twice. I grabbed two of my muskets, one in my left hand and the other in my right.

As they came toward me, I fired both guns at the same time. The volley terrified the group of men, and it was immediately clear to me that they had never seen a gun, or heard one fired before.

I guessed that these primitive savages thought I was some sort of vengeful island spirit. In my days at sea, I'd heard of similar incidents amongst remote tribes who had never had contact with Europeans, and had never seen guns before.

The pursuers came to a dead halt, whimpering

Firing both guns

in fear. I burst out of the bushes and fired off another two shots, high in the air. I must have been a terrible sight, in my goatskin clothing, waving my smoking firearms at the men. The cannibals screamed and turned to run.

Two of the men fell face-down in the sand, but their companions were too frightened to stop and help them.

I picked up two more muskets and fired again, into the sand close to the fallen men. Screaming, they struggled to their feet and ran on.

When the group of men reached their canoes, they leapt aboard and rowed for their lives. I could have loaded my muskets again and scared them still farther. But I had punished them enough, and they would tell any others still at home what had happened.

I doubted I would ever see any of them on my island again. With luck, they would think the island was haunted, and steer well clear of it in future.

I watched them until they vanished into the distance and then decided to follow the man who had escaped.

I had learned quite a lot about tracking animals during my stay on the island. I found it even easier to follow a man's tracks.

I soon picked up his direction. I followed his path right across the island. I was pleased to discover that he was heading straight back toward my castle.

I finally came face-to-face with him by my castle camp.

Chapter 20
Man Friday

The man I had rescued was a young native of about eighteen years old. He was a tall lad with long, powerful arms and legs. His hair was long and black, and he stared at me with large dark eyes.

He was terrified out of his wits. Yet, I was sure that in some way he knew I had saved his life on Footprint Beach.

With a smile on my face, I made signs for him to come forward. He understood this and stepped a little closer. Then he stopped. I smiled again, trying to encourage him. This time he came right up to me and sank to his knees, with his head on the ground.

I indicated for him to get up. I held out my hand for him to shake. He did not understand what I meant, so I took his right hand in mine and shook it up and down. Then I smiled and tried to show him that he could be my friend.

I shook his hand.

He must have understood something of what I meant. He started talking in some foreign language. I could not understand a word of what he said.

You cannot imagine how wonderful it was to hear another human voice. I smiled and shook his hand again. Then he smiled and shook my hand.

I decided to trust him. I presented him with one of my cutlasses, waiting a little nervously to see if he would try to attack me. Of course, he didn't. He smiled and twirled it about playfully, before proudly tucking it into the belt around his loincloth.

He smiled again and spoke more words. From his expression, he seemed to be saying that he understood he was my servant now. He shook my hand once more and knelt down in front of me again.

That evening as the sun set, I gave him some bread and raisins to eat, and a mug of cool water to drink. Then I handed him a thick blanket and pointed to a place at the back of my tent. I indicated that he was to sleep there.

He was happy to lie down and cover himself with the blanket. He was soon fast asleep.

The lad was still asleep the next morning

when I got up. As soon as he awoke, he started to follow me about, as if he was awaiting orders. I realized that he would make a wonderful helper for me.

Later, he came to the farm with me and watched as I milked the goats. He pointed excitedly at the goats and then at himself. I knew exactly what he was saying to me. He was showing me that he could milk goats.

So I gave him a bucket. I have to admit that he was better at milking than me. He was much quicker, and smiled proudly after finishing each goat.

I gave him some of my bread and cheese for breakfast, and sat him down outside the tent. I wanted to teach him some first words in English.

The first word I taught him was *Governor*. I pointed at myself and said the word over and over again. It didn't take him long to understand that I was to be called *Governor* and was to be obeyed.

Next I gave him a name. I had decided to call him Man Friday. That was the day on which I had met him. Again, it didn't take him long to understand his new name. He was very intelligent and quick to learn.

By the end of that first day he understood

Friday loved his new clothes.

the words *yes* and *no* and could ask for *water,* *bread,* and *cheese.*

The next day I made Friday some clothes to wear. I gave him a pair of sailor's breeches and a goatskin jacket. I also found him one of my goatskin caps. Friday loved his new clothes.

I made a small tent that I put up close to mine. Friday liked his new home and indicated to me that if anyone came into the camp, he would defend me.

As the days passed, I realized what a good servant I had found. He was faithful, honest, and loving. Sometimes I felt he was more like a brother to me that a servant.

Chapter 21
Life with Friday

I was delighted with Friday and made it my job to teach him as much as I could.

I taught him to use a hammer and saw. He quickly took to sewing and making clothes from goat skins. It wasn't long before Friday could make bread and cheese, too.

I taught him to shoot with a musket and pistol. He was terrified at first, when the gunpowder ignited and exploded. Like the cannibals at Footprint Beach, he'd never seen firearms before. But he quickly got used to them.

Friday learned new words every day. Soon we could almost have a conversation of sorts.

***

That first year with Friday was the happiest time I had spent on the island. And by the end of it, he could speak English almost fluently.

One day, on top of Beacon Hill, he pointed to the speck of land on the western horizon. He made it clear to me that it was his island home.

Friday was also able to tell me how two tribes lived there. There was his own people, and another more powerful race, the cannibals, who were his sworn enemy.

That tribe had murdered many of his people. He told me they sometimes brought their captives to my island and killed them here. It was a ceremonial place for them.

Teaching Friday as much as I could

119

He pointed to Footprint Beach, where the cannibals had been. "Them bad people," he said. "They would kill me. You saved me."

Now, for the first time, I was beginning to think that perhaps I might find a way to get home to England.

If the cannibals from Friday's island could row across to Crusoe Island, then surely I could do it in reverse. I asked Friday how long it might take. What he said gave me great excitement.

Friday spread his arms out. "Four days to Orinoco; one more to my island."

At last, I had a real clue to where I was! Friday must be talking about the Orinoco River. It flowed out of South America into the sea near the West Indies.

I asked Friday whether the sea between my island and his was dangerous.

"Many drown," he answered. "But can be done."

Later that evening, I told him my full story; how my father had warned me against going to sea and how I had ignored his advice. I told him how I was just seventeen when I was ship-wrecked on the island, and how much I missed my own people.

By the time I had finished my story the sun

"Four days to Orinoco; one more to my island."

had long gone and the only light that remained was a pale pink streak in the western sky.

That speck of light caught a tear in Friday's eye. He was sorry that I had spent so long on the island alone, and he gave me a comforting smile.

Friday had become a wonderful friend to me.

Chapter 22
Friday's Sad Story

Now I knew where I was, I supposed there was no real reason why I shouldn't set off in my boat and try to reach Friday's island.

But something told me not to. Firstly, I was sure another English ship might pass the island one day. Secondly, I was reluctant to sail out into the open ocean. The last time I'd done so, I had been terrified by awful storms, captured by pirates, and shipwrecked.

So I was prepared to wait a little longer before I risked my life again.

Friday seemed to enjoy his life with me. For the next year I gave him daily English and arithmetic lessons. He was a quick learner.

I also taught him about the continent of Europe and the island of Britain. I told him how we sailed our ships around the world, trading with other countries.

Some evenings I would talk about my family, especially my father.

I saw that Friday would usually fall silent when I mentioned my father and I asked him what the matter was.

"My father," said Friday, "was captured by our enemies. So he is dead now for sure. It makes me sad."

A few months later, I took Friday to the top of Beacon Hill again. He always became very excited when he went up there. He would point to the speck of land and cry out, "My island!"

I asked him whether he would like to go home.

"I cannot swim that far," he laughed. He had a good sense of humor.

"I know that," I smiled in return. "No—in my boat."

Friday said that he would go home, as long as I came with him.

"You will be our brother," he said, "I will tell my people how you saved my life."

That day I made the decision to leave Crusoe Island. We set about preparing my boat for its journey.

I spent several weeks teaching Friday how to steer and sail the boat. We were both becoming more and more excited as the day for our leaving came closer. Friday had now been with

"My father was captured by our enemies."

me for three years. I was sure he longed to return to his people.

We waited patiently for the quiet weather that would arrive in the month of December. All was going well until the morning Friday came rushing back from Beacon Hill.

"Canoes!" he cried. "Canoes coming!"

I scurried up the hill to see for myself. Using my telescope, I could make out seven or eight canoes.

I guessed that, somehow, the cannibals had learned I was not a vengeful spirit, but merely a man with guns. Now they were returning in greater numbers than before to take their revenge on me!

I decided it was time to teach the cannibals a lesson once and for all. This time, I would show them no mercy.

I had no choice—it was our lives or theirs. So Friday and I prepared to set sail for Footprint Beach.

Teaching Friday how to sail the boat

Chapter 23
Battle with the Savages

Thank goodness I had taught my faithful friend Friday to use my weapons.

"We must fight to the death now," I told Friday, as we neared Footprint Beach, "for they won't be scared of me this time."

"I stand beside you!" he answered boldly. "You saved my life. We are brothers in arms."

I quickly divided up between us the most deadly weapons I had.

Friday had three muskets hanging from his shoulder and two loaded pistols in his belt. He carried spare bags of gunpowder and shot too.

I was armed exactly the same as Friday, except that I managed to find space on my belt for a cutlass and dagger.

"Right my loyal friend!" I cried. "Now we'll show them."

We launched the boat and quickly sailed around to the headland by the western shore.

By the time we reached Footprint Beach, the canoes were just a little way offshore.

We ran up the beach to take up the same position I had when I had surprised the cannibals last time. I told Friday not to shoot at anyone or anything until I told him.

The visitors left their canoes on the shoreline and walked up the beach. There were about twenty of them, and they all carried spears.

They stopped some twenty yards from our position and prepared a large fire. It roared into life.

"Are you ready, Friday?" I whispered.

He nodded.

"Just do exactly what I do," I said.

I slipped my three muskets off my shoulder and lined them up against the bough of a tree. I picked up the first musket and took aim.

Friday did the same.

"Now Friday," I said. "When I say fire, we're going to shoot off all three guns in quick succession."

"I understand," said Friday, sounding a little anxious.

I took one last look at our targets. "Fire!" I cried.

I saw the savages turn to look at what was

"Are you ready, Friday?"

happening. It was too late for them. I hit one of them with my first shot. Friday jumped in delight when his own target tumbled to the ground.

We fired our second guns. Two more fell to earth. Friday had become a remarkable shot. The shots from the third guns brought down two more and scattered the rest of them.

Those still alive ran up and down the beach, not knowing where to go to escape our deadly fire.

While I continued firing with my three pistols, Friday reloaded all six muskets.

By the time the savages had stopped panicking and headed for their canoes to escape, we were ready again.

Six more volleys rang out from the wood. Six more savages fell to earth.

Of the twenty who had come ashore, only five now remained alive.

Four of them got away in another canoe but in their panic, capsized. I never saw what happened to them, but they must have drowned.

The last man escaped in his canoe.

"Cease fire!" I cried to Friday. "Leave the last man. Let him tell your enemies what happened today. They'll never come here again."

"Fire!"

What a day it had been. We had certainly destroyed a large number of Friday's enemies.

But the day wasn't over yet. Friday was about to have the surprise of his life.

Chapter 24

A Great Surprise

We buried the bodies and then searched the canoes the savages had left behind. I was astounded to find another person still alive at the bottom of one of them. He had been tied up from head to toe, so tightly that he hadn't been able to move.

I called to Friday to help me free him. When Friday looked inside he let out a great cry. I did not understand the word he used. But then he turned to me and said one word in English: "Father!"

I could hardly believe it. We had found Friday's father. We immediately cut him free and poured some water down his throat.

At last he sat up. It would have moved anyone to tears to see how Friday hugged him.

We pulled Friday's father from the boat and sat him down on the beach. He was exhausted from the terrors he had been through. Friday

We had found Friday's father.

brought some raisins and bread from our boat for him to eat.

That evening the three of us sailed back to Castle Crusoe. Friday's father was soon fast asleep in my tent.

I stayed awake for a long time that night, thinking how strange it was that after all these years I was no longer alone. My island now had three people living on it!

Friday made his father a large goat meat stew when he awoke the next day, and the older man quickly began to regain his strength.

For myself, I was anxious to learn from Friday's father whether he thought his captors would return to attack us. Friday acted as his interpreter.

It seemed he thought that we had given the savages such a beating that the one who had escaped would certainly warn them against coming back. Besides, he said, we had killed the best of the savage warriors.

Friday's father also had a most interesting piece of news. An English man-of-war had dropped anchor by his island. He said that seventeen English sailors had come ashore.

My heart leapt with excitement. I decided that I had to sail across as soon as possible now.

But once more all my plans came to nothing.

That evening, Friday ran down from Beacon Hill shouting in excitement, "Big boat coming!"

We all raced up the hill. I expected to see more canoes coming, but there were none. Instead, I saw a large man-of-war was approaching the island. I immediately saw the flag on her mast. She was an English ship!

Friday's father indicated that this was the same ship that he had seen anchored off his

Friday acted as his interpreter.

island.

The ship dropped anchor almost opposite the creek that led to my castle. We watched as a small boat was launched.

You cannot imagine the excitement I felt to see an English ship. I wanted to run down to the beach shouting for joy. Yet, something told me that all wasn't right. It was just instinct. I stayed on the hill and watched, as the small boat reached shore.

There were six men on the boat. Four men got out first, and then hauled out two more. I was shocked to see that these men had their hands tied behind their backs.

I was even more astonished to see that the two men were wearing the uniforms of English naval officers. I wasn't quite sure what to do now. I told Friday and his father to follow me back to the camp.

Back at Castle Crusoe, I thought how glad I was that I had built my defenses, for we were well hidden.

The sailors had walked their prisoners down the creek and now stood just a few yards from my overgrown stockade. They had no idea that I was just a few feet away from them. I heard their every word.

Chapter 25
The Mutiny

The four men were jeering at their captives.

"How do you like your new home, Captain?" said one. "You'll never see England again."

"I'll be home in time to see you mutineers hanged," replied the man, who I took to be captain of the English ship.

"You'll never get off this island once we've gone," cried the second man.

Now I knew what was going on. The ship's crew had mutinied, and their hideous plan was to maroon the captain and the other officer on my island.

"Tie the officers to a tree," ordered the man who was clearly the leader of the mutineers. "We'll come back when we've found some fresh water for the ship. This creek's too salty."

They tied the officers securely to a nearby tree and went off on their search.

Once they were gone, I hurriedly used the ladders to clamber over the defenses. Friday

Tying the officers to a tree

and his father followed.

The captain and his fellow officer were shocked at the sight of my companions and I. The blood drained from the captain's face. He went quite ashen. I think they both expected to be killed on the spot.

"Gentlemen," I said, lifting my cap. "At your service."

The captain stared at me in astonishment. He couldn't speak for a moment.

"Are you English?" he asked at last, trying to see what man it was who lay behind the huge beard covering most of my face.

"I am English, sir!" I cried. "Robinson Crusoe, lately of the English town of Hull. And this is my servant, Man Friday, and his father."

"Free us, man!" cried the captain, recovering his wits at last. "Free us before they get back! I am Captain Nathan of Her Majesty's Ship *Norfolk*. And this is First Officer Jones."

Friday quickly cut their ropes.

"My men have mutinied," explained Captain Nathan. "They planned to maroon us on this island and leave us to die."

I told them to follow me over the ladders. Once safely inside, we brought the ladders in and I ordered Friday to load all the muskets, and set them ready to be fired through the holes in the stockade.

I handed Captain Nathan and his First Officer a loaded musket and pistol.

Half an hour later we heard the sound of footsteps returning through the undergrowth, and we raised our muskets, ready to fire.

The four men emerged from the bushes and walked into the clearing in front of my camp. I saw the puzzled look on their faces as they searched for their prisoners.

"They've escaped!" shouted one man.

"Nonsense!" cried their leader. "We must have got the wrong place."

"No," said another, "here's the tree we tied them to."

"It's magic!" said the fourth man. "Let's get out of here."

"There's no magic here," said the leader, walking up to the tree. "The ropes have been cut. See!"

He held up the ropes to show the others.

That was the moment Captain Nathan barked out an order to the men, from behind the stockade. "Stand where you are! You are under arrest for mutiny! One move and you are all dead men!"

"My men have mutinied."

Through the holes in the stockade and over-growth beyond, I saw the leader's face turn white with shock.

The captain's voice must have sounded as if it came out of the trees. The mutineers looked in our direction but could still not see us, although we were just feet away.

"I'm getting out of here!" one cried. "The place is spooked."

All four turned and ran back toward the boat on the beach.

"Stop where you are or we'll fire!" shouted the captain.

The mutineers refused to listen and kept running.

That was the moment the captain gave the order. "Fire!"

The mutineers turned just in time to see four muskets appear through the bushes and stockade that hid us so well.

The explosion of gunpowder was the last thing the villains saw. The four died instantly.

Chapter 26
Ten Mutineers

That evening, Friday and his father cooked a delicious meal of roast goat for us, as I told my story to the captain.

"Why, you've been here sixteen years!" he exclaimed. He was astounded that I had been trapped on the island for so many years.

"Yes, I was just a boy of seventeen years when I was shipwrecked," I said. "Now I am a man of thirty-two."

I had so many questions I wanted to ask the captain about what had happened in England since I left. We talked long into the night.

The last thing we discussed was how we would capture the other mutineers still aboard the ship.

"We've killed the ringleaders," he said. "The others shouldn't cause us too much trouble."

But before we went to sleep that night, I put Friday on guard by the stockade, just in case.

He woke us at dawn to say he had been on Beacon Hill and seen a boat carrying ten mutineers leave the ship. They were obviously coming to see why their leaders hadn't returned.

We were ready for them when they walked into the clearing.

"Give them a few barrels of shot over their heads," ordered Captain Nathan. "That'll keep them quiet!"

We all fired our muskets. A ferocious volley of musket and pistol shot fizzed above them. The mutineers were so surprised that they dropped to the ground in terror.

Moments later we emerged from behind the stockade. They were astonished to see their two officers with us.

They hadn't even bothered to arm themselves. They had thought the island uninhabited, and they never imagined that the captain and first officer could have overpowered the ringleaders.

I had never seen a sadder bunch of young men. They were terrified. They knew that mutiny was a hanging offence.

They begged for their lives, but the captain said the law of mutiny demanded they be hanged. He would have hanged them then and

I put Friday on guard, just in case.

there, but the first officer said they should be sent back to England for trial in London.

All those men knew what that meant. They would swing on a rope as well in London as they would on Crusoe Island.

I felt sorry for them now. They were just poor innocents caught up in the mutiny.

"Captain," I said, "have you no pity for these men? Didn't I save your lives? Didn't we kill the ringleaders? Surely we can show mercy to these men."

The captain was not a cruel man. He said he did have some sympathy for the men, but had no power to pardon them.

"I have an idea, Captain," I said. "Don't forget you are on my island. Many years ago I claimed this land on behalf of my country. Indeed, I appointed myself Governor some years ago."

"He is Governor Crusoe," said Man Friday.

"He is Governor Crusoe," mimicked Poll, who had just fluttered down onto my shoulder.

The captain thought for a moment and then gave his answer. "I accept that perhaps you are the rightful Governor of the island for now. But even a governor cannot pardon mutiny, Mr. Crusoe."

"No," I replied, "but I have an idea."

I had never seen a sadder bunch.

Robinson Crusoe

The captain wanted to know what my plan was, but I wasn't ready to tell him yet.

There was something else to do first. We had to recapture the ship from the remaining mutineers still aboard.

Chapter 27
An Early Morning Raid

The first part of my plan involved talking secretly to the ten mutineers we had captured.

"Would you like to make amends for your mutiny?" I asked the men who were now detained under the careful eye of Man Friday and his loaded musket.

To a man they answered, "Aye!"

"Then will you come with the captain, first officer, Mr. Friday, and myself, and help to recapture the ship?"

Once more they cried, "Aye!"

"If you do this," I said, "then I promise you will not hang. You have my word."

Then I told the captain that the men had agreed to help us take back the ship.

"A fine idea," said the captain, "but how will we do it?"

"Trust me," I said. "We'll strike when they least expect it. And the sooner we regain the ship, the quicker we'll all be back in England."

The next morning before dawn, we marched our prisoners down to the beach and loaded them onto the same boat they had arrived on.

I ordered the mutineers to sit at the front of the boat. The captain, first officer, myself, and Friday with his father sat at the back. We covered them with our muskets and pistols, just in case they tried anything.

With the sun still below the horizon, I asked the mutineers to row us out to the ship. There was not a sound coming from it. As we came closer, I saw a guard had been left on the side of the ship facing the island.

He heard our boat coming through the water.

"Who goes there?" he called, peering out through the dim first light of day. "Friend or foe?"

"Friend!" I called, pretending to be one of the mutineers. "We're back. Captain Nathan and First Officer Jones have been well and truly marooned. They'll never be seen again. They'll be dead in months."

"Good work, me old shipmates," cried the guard, dropping a rope ladder over the side.

I whispered to the sailors to climb aboard. "But remember, I'm right behind you!" I added, poking one man in the back with my musket.

An Early Morning Raid

Rowing out to the ship

They climbed aboard with Friday and I hidden among them. The captain and first officer followed.

I whispered something in Friday's ear, giving him a job to do.

He didn't hesitate. He crept up behind the guard and gave him a sharp blow on the head with the wooden end of his musket. The guard fell to the floor, unconscious.

The sleeping ship was ours! Everyone else was still snoring below decks.

Next, I gave the first officer a job to do. He went up to the ship's bell and gave it five great clangs. Five bells told the ship's crew it was time to rise for the morning watch.

Now, we lined up our men on the front deck of the ship and hid ourselves behind them.

One by one all the other mutineers came on deck. They were a little puzzled when they saw their friends lined up on the deck.

"What's up, mates?" asked one.

"This is what's up, mates," I said, stepping through the line of sailors with my friends.

The men saw our loaded muskets and pistols. Their jaws dropped in surprise. Each one felt the hangman's noose rubbing around his neck.

I sent Friday down to disarm them.

"Put one foot wrong and I swear I will hang every one of you right now," roared Captain Nathan.

Once we had their weapons, I told the ten mutineers we had arrived with to join their friends. Only then did I reveal the final part of my plan to everyone.

The sleeping ship was ours!

Chapter 28
Live or Die!

I climbed up to the top deck and turned to speak to the mutineers.

"To those who don't know me, I am Governor of Crusoe Island," I began, " and I'm going to give you all the chance of life or death."

There was a sudden hush. I spoke again. "Your first choice is to return with us to England and face trial for mutiny."

I saw their faces drop. There wasn't a man there who didn't know what that meant; a certain meeting with the hangman.

"What's our other choice?" cried one sailor.

"The law against mutineers is very tough," I replied, "but I don't think any of you deserve to die. The ringleaders you so foolishly followed are dead. I'm giving you the chance to make amends for your mistake. So the choice is yours: to live or die."

"I want to live," said a young sailor at the front. "I am my mother's only son. It would

Speaking to the mutineers

break her heart if I died."

Then came other voices, all pleading to be allowed to live.

"You haven't told us what we have to do to stay alive," said a rough old sea dog.

"If you listen, I will tell you," I said, looking at the desperate faces all around me. "I want you to stay behind and live on Crusoe Island."

There was another sudden hush that was only broken by the voice of the old sea dog. "That's as good as hanging us all," he said. "If you maroon us all here, we'll die of starvation or be eaten by cannibals."

I went on to explain a few things about the island none of them yet knew.

"You will never starve or die of thirst on Crusoe Island," I said. "Tomorrow I will take you to Valley Farm. It's my farm on the island, and it is already producing fruit, vegetables, and corn for bread flour. I also have a flock of goats for milk and meat.

"I have already built a small settlement there beside the river. It would take nothing for you to build a few wooden huts to live in. Then you could work on the farm and grow all the food you need. You could sell your crops to visiting ships or even some of it to England."

The sailors were listening closely now, and I saw the light of hope in their eyes.

"Some of you know already that I also have a comfortable camp called Castle Crusoe near the coast," I continued. "I have spent many years there alone. But if you stay here, you won't be alone and you won't want for anything. My boat is yours to patrol the coast and warn off any unwanted visitors."

The sailors started excitedly talking to each other.

"You mean," said the old sea dog, "that we can make it our own little country . . . elect a leader . . . run it ourselves."

"Not so much your country," I answered, "but a new English colony that you would develop. We'll leave behind all the things you need, such as muskets and powder, and as much food as we can spare.

"And I, as Governor, would visit you now and again to see how you are managing."

The captain was delighted. "A marvelous plan, Mr. Crusoe!"

He turned to the men. "It's time to vote on Mr. Crusoe's plan. All those in favor, raise your hands."

Not one man voted against the idea.

"A marvelous plan, Mr. Crusoe."

"So be it!" cried the captain.

He then went on to explain that he would need a few of the men to help sail the ship back to England. He chose several who he knew were unhappy about the mutiny, but had been forced to go along with it.

I was glad that everyone had agreed to my plan. But I felt a little sad, now that I realized my life on the island was coming to an end. I desperately wanted to return home, but part of me now belonged to Crusoe Island forever.

I knew that once I got back to England, I would soon be dreaming of my next visit to the island.

Chapter 29
Farewell to the Island

For the next few days we ferried all the men's possessions ashore, along with large quantities of food, muskets and powder, and tools. I showed them all over my island. By the time it came for us to go, they all seemed reasonably happy with their lot.

The captain cheered the men up when he told them they should keep a watchman on Beacon Hill every day. "You will not be alone, as Mr. Crusoe was. English ships will regularly call here now. And later, perhaps your wives and sweethearts might be allowed to join you."

And so the time came to leave. I spent the last day visiting all my regular haunts, my farm, the castle, and Beacon Hill.

On the hill, I looked once more at the speck of land that I had I stared at for so many years.

Just then, I saw my boat setting sail from the headland by Footprint Beach. Two of the men had volunteered to take Friday's father back to his own island.

Friday couldn't bear to be parted from me, so it had been agreed that I would take him to England.

I walked slowly over to Rosie's grave. "I'll be back my beauty," I said, with a tear in my eye.

"I'll be back my beauty," echoed Poll.

Back at the castle, I loaded my possessions onto one of Captain Nathan's boats. The most precious item of all was my calendar post.

I made one last notch at five o'clock that afternoon. It was Christmas Eve 1668. The post reminded me that I had been on the island for sixteen years.

I went aboard the ship still wearing my oldest possession; the beard I had grown on the island. The ship's barber gave me a much-needed shave, just before we set sail.

"Raise anchor!" cried the captain. "Raise the mainsail! Set course for England!"

The chains clanked as the anchor freed itself. The warm evening breeze filled the sails. We began to move.

I saw the sun set behind the island as we sailed east.

I was going home at last!

I had been on the island for sixteen years.

Chapter 30
Home at Last

So together with Friday and Poll the parrot, I made the journey home.

It took us a month to reach England. How strange it was to see my homeland again. After all the years that had passed, it seemed like a foreign land.

Man Friday, now dressed in a navy uniform given to him by Captain Nathan, was like an excited child.

He couldn't believe his eyes when he saw the city of London and the busy streets. It snowed in the city while we were there. Friday was so surprised, because he had never seen snow before.

We didn't stay in London long; we quickly took a coach to Hull, from where I had set sail all those years before.

There, my worst fears were confirmed. My parents had died several years earlier. But I did find my sister still alive. She told me that I had long been given up for dead by most people, but my father never gave up hope.

"He left you a message on his deathbed," she said. "He said that he had forgiven you for running away to sea."

My father had left me a little money, too. I used it to start a small shipping company with Captain Nathan and Man Friday.

How strange it was to see my homeland again.

We bought a ship which I named *Rosie*, after my dog. We used the ship to trade in the Caribbean, including, of course, Crusoe Island itself.

The island produced large quantities of oranges and coconuts for wealthy customers in London.

All three of us became quite rich. Yet I could see that Friday was never completely happy living in England. After five years he told me that he wanted to return to his homeland.

I knew I would miss Friday's company, but I agreed that he should return, if it would make him happier. He was to travel home on our ship. I decided to go with him to see how Crusoe Island had changed.

When we arrived, I hardly recognized the place. The creek that led from the beach to my camp had been widened and made deeper. There was now a small quay for ships to tie up to, right beside where my first home had been.

The stockade had gone. The whole area had become a small harbor settlement with lots of tiny wooden cottages and narrow lanes. There was even a small church and meeting house.

We went to see my farm in the valley. There were lots more fields now, and big new orchards of oranges and coconuts.

I climbed Beacon Hill once more and looked out to that speck of land on the horizon. Friday was so excited to see his homeland again, especially now that he knew he would be back there in a few days time.

I was so pleased to see that the mutineers we had left behind had tended Rosie's grave.

The men there thanked me for giving them the chance to stay on the island, rather than face the gallows in England. Several had become quite rich through trading with my shipping company.

They had now received pardons for their past sins, but most had still decided to stay on in the island. Their wives, mothers, and families had been able to join them.

It was a joy to see very young children running around the lanes. I noticed that a school was already being built for them.

We stayed for a few days and then traveled on to Friday's home. We found his father still alive and well, and I was treated to a wonderful feast by Friday's family.

The next day Friday and I said our sad farewells. But I told him I would be back to visit him again soon.

The voyage back to England was uneventful

I hardly recognized the place.

and we made it to Hull in under a month.

And so, I grew richer. I built a large house for myself, and soon after, I married and had a beautiful daughter and a son. My son grew into a fine, adventurous young lad. He reminded me of myself in my younger days.

It came as no surprise to me when he began spending hours by the harbor in Hull, watching all the ships come and go. It was also no surprise when he told his mother and I that he wanted to leave home, and sail the seven seas.

I understood how he felt, but I did take him aside and give him a warning.

"Young Master Crusoe," I said in my sternest voice, "nothing but disaster will come of it. Take a good office job in town, my boy. That's the place for you. Go to sea and you'll be shipwrecked in some uncharted land, and be eaten by wild beasts or cannibals."

Do you think he listened to my advice?

The End